G000124074

EMBRACE THE DARKNESS
and other short stories

ISBN: 1548536407

ISBN-13: 978-1548536404

For my Leanne and her 'horror Tourettes'

ABOUT THE AUTHOR

This is the debut anthology from author Peter Blakey-Novis. Peter lives with his wife and four children in a small town in Sussex, England. As well as being a keen cook and wine enthusiast, Peter has been writing poetry and short stories for almost twenty years. An excitement for literature and storytelling has led to Peter now about to publish his second novel, as well as this range of short stories. Peter has also written children's stories, aimed specifically for his own children, currently close to being published.

KEEP UP TO DATE!

More information about the author can be found on his website as well as social media profiles listed below. You can also subscribe to the email mailing list via the website for exciting news about future releases, as well as accessing short stories direct to your mailbox! If you have any comments or would like to just get in touch feel free to email directly at the address below. Happy reading!

Twitter: www.twitter.com/pjbn_author
Facebook: www.facebook.com/pjbnauthor
Web: www.pjbnauthor.wordpress.com
Email: pjblakey-novis@outlook.com
Subscribe: www.patreon.com/pjbnauthor

CONTENTS;

ABANDONMENT

"I told you I would never leave you," Marcus said, his eyes red from tears. "I don't understand why you would think that I would." Alice looked at him, sadly. He looked upset, frightened, as he sat on the floor in the corner of their bedroom. "I don't understand what's happening."

"I love you," she told him, with complete and unwavering certainty. "I need to tell you some things about my life; things that I have not told you before, not in any detail anyway."

"You can tell me anything, you know that," Marcus replied, his voice trembling.

"I guess I'm worried about frightening you away, but I need to get it all out. I just can't risk you leaving me. Even so, here it goes." There was a heavy silence as Alice looked Marcus straight in the eye. "They all left. Eventually," she continued. "Some would just grow distant, gradually and over a long period of time. Some were gone in an instant, with the slamming of a door or, in one case, opting for the afterlife. For the thirty years that I've been alive, I have never been able to understand what I was supposed to do with my life. It is only now that I'm starting to take on board what has happened to me, to begin to comprehend why I feel the way I do. And to write my list."

"What list?" Marcus asked from his position

upon the floor. His voice was quiet, sensing that something was wrong.

"The list of people who have left me. I don't want you to be on the list, Marcus. That cannot happen." Marcus nodded. "The first person to go had been my own mother (number 1) but as I was only two years old at the time, I really have very little recollection of the incident. Even now, the circumstances around her abandonment of me are unclear, and I do have the sense to know that there was likely to be more to it than what my father had let on. It had been him that had raised me, along with my sister, as you know." Again, Marcus nodded, already vaguely aware of Alice's upbringing. "My father had struggled. And when I was still at primary school my grandmother (number 2 on the list), the only female role model whom I had, committed suicide. It was shocking for everyone, causing arguments and blame to be thrown about the family, but I was too young to make any sense of it, knowing only that my grandma was now gone as well." This was new information for Marcus, and he looked surprised and saddened.

"Sorry," was all he could manage, watching as Alice paced the room.

"It was not until I became a teenager that I thought more about the people missing from my life and, more importantly, why they were not there for me. This is when things had begun to hurt, as though their departure was a direct rejection of me. I mean, if they cared about me, then they would have stuck around, right?

My father had tried his best to raise my sister and me as strong, independent young women but, certainly for me, this had backfired. I became too independent, unreasonably headstrong, clashing with my father and sister more and more often. There was no way of controlling me, no form of discipline that he attempted to use would make any difference. He would hit me over the slightest thing but this only served to push me further away, so I'd act more recklessly, until one day I left." Alice's voice had risen as she spoke of the physical punishments that her father had dealt out, angry now that he had dared to hit her. Thinking back, Alice couldn't remember what the fight was about on the day that she had left, but she could still see him clearly, standing in the hallway between their living room and kitchen. He had told her that if she didn't like it there, then she should leave. And so she did.

"This was the point of no return; you see. My pride being too much to think of going back. At sixteen, I found work and a place to live. It was just a room in someone's house, but it was clean, and I was out most of the time. The period of adjustment was fairly short lived, managing to get myself into a healthy routine of eating and keeping my clothes washed. It felt like an adventure, with the freedom to do as I pleased masking the pain of being thrown into the world at too young an age. How old were you when you left home?" Alice asked Marcus, staring at him in a way that unsettled him.

"Erm, eighteen I think, when I went to uni."

"I guess that's quite normal. It must have been nice to leave of your own accord; I felt pushed out. Suddenly, I found that I had a lot of so-called friends, all wanting to stay over as they all still lived with their parents. I would visit my father (number 3 on my list) and sister (number 4) less and less often, feeling more like an outsider with each visit. Can you believe that was fourteen years ago? I can still remember how things felt, how much it hurt. The signs were there, as clear as day for anyone else, but I was oblivious to them." Alice paused for a moment, thinking things over.

"What signs?" Marcus asked.

"That I have some issues," Alice told him, her tone suggesting that it was the most obvious thing in the world.

"I don't think you have issues. You've just been through some things."

"Well, we'll see if you still think that when I get near the end of my story," Alice told him, smiling sadly. "I met a boy whom I thought, certainly at that age, that I really liked, possibly even loved. We were together for a few months, and I would spend all of my time with him, not talking to anyone else. However, I would not sleep with him, and that was the problem.

Thinking back now, I don't know why I didn't just do it, but perhaps it had been a test to see if he would leave me. Eventually, he did (he's now number 5 on the list), and not just leave, but he started seeing my best friend, who it turned out was more 'up for it'. She is now number 6.

When I was not quite seventeen and, among the terror of hormones and adolescence, I felt alone, angry and lost. I'd reached my lowest point, and it had come suddenly, or at least, it had felt that way. There was nothing to fall back on, nothing to numb the hurt except to take it out on myself. I contemplated suicide but couldn't actually go through with it, so I started to cut myself." Alice stared at Marcus as she told him this, trying to work out what he thought of it. "You don't look surprised," she told him.

"I'm not stupid, Alice. I've seen the scars on your arms and legs."

"Yet you never asked about them." Alice sounded disappointed.

"I figured you'd tell me if you wanted me to know, like you are at the moment." Alice now thought back to those days, how low she had been and how close the end had seemed. Nevertheless, here she was, still alive.

"The next ten years or so feel like they flew by; I moved house often, changed jobs frequently. During nearly all of that time, I was not alone, and this now seems strange. Three relationships have filled the last ten years, interspersed with only a matter of months between them and a number of one-night stands. Matthew was the first long-term relationship, my longest at the time, anyway. Eighteen months with a guy a little younger than me, who seemed to worship me. I had moved more than sixty miles away to be with him, and it had been wonderfully exciting. Until it ended, out of the blue, by phone (Matthew is number 7). I never did see him again; I collected my belongings, whilst he was at work, but I still think about him sometimes, even now. He gave me no explanation, and it hurt, of course, but I coped well. I felt stronger at that time; I had a group of friends, and I was old enough to go out to bars and clubs, there were still people around. My mind had wandered back to cutting myself when he had left me, but I managed to resist, for the time being, at least."

"I got dumped after my first long-term relationship," Marcus pointed out. His tone was still friendly enough but Alice felt as though he were downplaying her sadness. "I know it hurts," he continued. "But you've got me now, I told you I'm sticking around."

"Six months later, I was in another relationship," Alice continued, not acknowledging what Marcus had told her. "This one was to be a real disappointment." Alice thought back to how things had been, how desperate she must have seemed at the start. "We had met at a bar, both drunk, and I had gone home with him. Thinking back now, I wonder how differently my life would have worked out if I just had not given him my number. After the first night he had called me, he wanted to see me again. And again. And again. It was nice to have the attention, and I didn't have much else to do, anyway. That was until I fell pregnant." Now there was a pause. Alice had never mentioned this crucial part of her life to anyone that was still around, but it was out now. Marcus kept a neutral expression in his face, only a slight flicker conveying surprise for just a moment.

"What happened?" he asked, presuming that Alice had opted for an abortion as there was clearly no child with her now.

"If my boyfriend had panicked, lost interest or simply bailed out, then perhaps I would not have kept going, but he was happy about the pregnancy and, therefore, so was I. The feelings I had for him were not strong, but they were, I had hoped, enough to hold things together. We had been with each other for a year when the baby came." A silence hung over them as Marcus tried to make sense of what he was being told. Alice pulled out some photographs from the inside pocket of a long coat which hung in their wardrobe, one that Marcus had never seen her wear. She showed Marcus a picture of a baby, only a few days old by the look of him.

"I thought, seeing him there, lying in that cot,

that this was someone who would never leave me. Six weeks after he had been born, we were shopping for tiny coffins (number 8 on my list, my own son)." Alice was struggling to hold back tears now, and Marcus was having the same problem. He had not expected this at all; neither could he imagine the pain that she carried. "That should have been the point at which we went on our separate ways," she told him. "Nevertheless, our grief held us together, neither of us wanting to abandon the other, both sharing in something that no-one else would be able to understand, not ever. The pain that had bound us soon began to tear us apart as we dealt with the loss in different ways. He carried on living his life, going to work, seeing his friends. It was as though he was over it, although I'm sure he wasn't really. He had loved me much more than I loved him, and if I'd stayed, then I think that it would have been enough for him to make it through. Even so, I couldn't stay, I never really had wanted to."

"So you left him?" Marcus asked.

"I had to. It wouldn't have been fair to stay, but it came hard, never having walked away from anyone in my life. I felt an enormous amount of guilt for abandoning him, the father of my lost child. Nevertheless, I just could not stay, not after what we had been through, wasting the years on someone who I took no pleasure in being with. It was terrifying; I was getting older and scared of being alone, but the constant stabs of deep pain throughout my life had numbed me to feel anything. *Things can't get worse,* I remember telling myself. *So, there's nothing more to be afraid of.* The numbness did not sit well and I tried to feel something, anything. I needed to find some kind of release. I became more and more distraught as I realized that nothing seemed to work; sleeping around did not make me feel anything, drugs were disappointing, alcohol only made me suicidal."

"I'm so sorry," Marcus told her, tears beginning to run down his cheeks. "You know I'm not going anywhere, though. Right?"

"That's what they've all said," Alice replied, sadly.

"Well, I mean it. I love you."

"You must think I'm crazy?"

"Not at all. I'm just so sorry that you've been through so much. However, it's in the past. We'll be alright."

"I'd understand if you wanted to leave me, I'm a mess!" Alice told him.

"Don't be so silly, I'm here to stay. You and I forever, that's what I told you. Just don't go doing anything stupid! I think it'll help for you to see someone, a professional, I mean. What do you think?"

"It's too late for all that," Alice told him, taking a seat next to him on the floor. "I just need you to decide what you want. You need to choose between staying with me or leaving, because if you are going to go, then please get it over with."

"I've already explained it so many times," Marcus said, trying not to sound irritated. "I want to be with you always; I mean it." Alice began to cry, conflicting emotions fighting in her head. The joy of Marcus promising her forever began clashing with her determination to leave this world, culminating in only one possible course of action.

"Then let's stay together until the end of time," Alice told him, leaning in to kiss him. Passionately and filled with emotion, Marcus kissed her back, absorbed in the moment. So absorbed, in fact, that he did not notice the glimmer of sunlight as it struck the silver blade of the scalpel. The first he knew of its presence was a sharp jab to his neck, his eyes widening as he watched thick spurts of blood spray across Alice's chest.

"Forever," she repeated, opening her wrists up in front of him and cradling his head as the life drained away. She had offered the chance for him to leave, but he wanted to stay. He had made his choice, and now no-one could ever leave her again.

BETRAYAL

There is a thin line between prophecy and witchcraft. The consequences for both could not be farther apart, however. This is something that I learned at a young age. My father was a farmer, still is I presume if he remains alive. My mother married him at just fifteen, almost twenty years his junior, common practice in these times. My father had been married previously but lost his first wife to a plague of sickness, which had swept through the village, taking more than half of the villagers with it. The loss was made doubly tragic as she had been pregnant with his first born but the way that I look at it, if she had survived, then I would not have existed.

Desperately lonely and in need of companionship, my parent's marriage was arranged only a few months later; my father determined to have someone bear him a son whom he could pass the farm on to. Perhaps he has one now; I do not know. It has been over ten years since I have seen him, over ten years since the trial - if you could call it that. My mother fell pregnant soon after they were married, understanding exactly what her role in life was to be. She knew no better and expected no more; content with becoming a farmer's wife and the bearer of his children.

Physically, my mother was not ready for

childbirth; her frame too slight to endure the strain that it would put on her. Had she fallen pregnant with one child then perhaps she would have survived, but twins were all too much. My sister was born first, by almost ten minutes, and it was clear to my father, as well as to those assisting in the birth, that all was not well. From what I have been told, which is not a great deal, my mother had lost consciousness by the time they managed to drag me out of her, bleeding profusely from the tears that we had caused. She never awoke, not living long enough to see her seventeenth birthday. My father was inconsolable, having buried two wives and gained no son in exchange for his loss.

As much as he had wanted a son, my father could not bring himself to remarry, unable to face the risk of losing a third wife. He accepted what he saw as his fate, solemnly moving on with his life at the farm, doing his best to raise two daughters alone. I remember him telling us that he did not want to send us off to be married, as was the custom for girls of a certain age. He wanted to prepare us for a life of farming, regardless of what anyone else would think. We looked up to him at that time, and from a very young age, we were taught everything that we would need to know in order to take over when my father was no longer able to tend to the fields himself.

The dreams began when we turned twelve. I

say we because my sister had the equivalent dreams, on the same nights. They were virtually identical visions with one crucial difference. I would dream that I had an important destiny, that I would, someday, rise to fame. That I was chosen by a higher power to pass on the prophecies to mortal men. In my dreams, my sister became a force for evil, choosing to live a life of witchcraft and heresy. There was a scene that kept running over, night after night, in which we were both surrounded by a mob of people from the neighbouring villages. The conversation within the dream was muffled, but it resulted in my sister being dragged to a stake, bound and burned alive. As close as we were in the real world, I appeared to feel no remorse in the dream. My sister's dream was identical, except that our roles were reversed, and I was the evil one.

We spent days working within the fields, talking about the dreams each night that we had them. After the first few nights, realizing that they were identical and had occurred simultaneously, we sought the advice of our father. He looked afraid as we explained, in a childlike way, what we had seen. *They are not dreams,* he had told us as we sat around the fire one evening. *They are visions. What you have seen will take place one day, I am sure of it.* He looked sad as he told us this, certain that he was to lose one of his daughters too. *You must stay at the farm, keep yourselves to yourselves. We will just have to see what happens.*

Those dreams had become less frequent, and we had all but forgot about them, by the time we had turned sixteen. My sister and I had had other dreams, of course, but they were nowhere near as vivid. We would dream the same things still, something my father put down to the closeness of our birth. It was only as we got older that we began to notice things, parts of our dreams edging their way into reality. We shared a vision of a storm, more violent than any we had experienced before. A few days later, the farm was hammered with a similar storm, torrential rain flooding the fields, lightning striking the farm equipment. We saw the deformed face of a traveler, who would come by a few weeks in the future looking for shelter. We awoke simultaneously, having envisaged the slaughter of my father's sheep, only to find their carcasses scattered across the field, victims of wolves.

My father played it down, trying to explain away the occurrences, fearful, perhaps, of our power. The vision that changed everything came when we saw the funeral of one of the village elders, a much loved and revered leader. Everyone was gathered around his coffin, leaving flowers and sobbing, his body covered with a white sheet to conceal the gruesome wounds that he had suffered. Personally, I had not considered taking any action about the dream, not knowing what we could possibly have done. My sister, on the other hand, was insistent that we must warn the villagers. *We could save his life!* she urged. My father forbade it. *It's too dangerous if you tell the people, and if something then happens to him, they will blame you! They'll charge you with heresy!*

I accepted my father's ruling and knew better than to disobey him. My sister, however, was far more rebellious than I. Following a terrible argument between my father and my sister, she had waited until we were all asleep before making the trek into the village. She managed to return before either of us could become suspicious, and it was not for another week that we would discover what she had done. It was a hot afternoon when they came, armed with whatever makeshift weapons they had been able to find. As the mob progressed along the dusty track at the edge of my father's land, he sensed that something was wrong, ushering us into the house. From where we sat, hands trembling, peeking through the curtains, we could not make out what was being said - merely that there was an angry discussion taking place.

After a few moments, my father was knocked to the ground, a scythe placed at his throat. Helplessly he watched as they came for us, binding our hands with coarse ropes and marching us into the village. That was the last time that I saw him, lying there, sobbing as we left. I can only assume that he knew what would become our fate and could not bring himself to come and watch. The villagers had clearly been talking about us, working each other up into a frenzy. We were both pelted with rotten fruit and stones as we were led to the village square. That was when everything became clear. As I gazed down on the coffin of the village elder, identical to how he had appeared in my dream, I knew what my sister had done. I felt an anger rise up within me, staring at her, eyes beginning to well up. As good as her intentions may have been, she had been unable to prevent the man's murder.

The villagers formed a circle around us as we stood, a stake having been erected near the centre of the village square. It seemed as though they had already made up their mind. The scene came flooding back to me, just as it had been in the visions of my twelve-year-old self. There was a look of recognition on my sister's face as well, a familiarity with the setting. Nevertheless, her dream had been different; I recalled. There was no way to know yet whose version was accurate. The remaining elders began their speech, citing witchcraft as the reason for our arrest.

You came here, one of you, predicting the murder of our great leader. If you possessed the power to foresee this terrible event, why did you not take steps to prevent it? There was a jeer from the crowd. My sister just looked at me, unsure of how to reply, trying her best not to cry. I remained silent.

Which one of you was it? Speak now or you shall both be charged!

It was me, my sister began. *I brought warning so that it could be avoided. I tried to help you! We both had the same visions; it is not witchcraft. It's a gift!*

A gift? came a voice from the crowd. *We are not to know the future; it is heresy!*

Is it true? the elder asked, looking at me. *You both have these visions?* I will never forget the look on my sister's face as I denied my gift, as I pleaded that I knew nothing of what she spoke, that I was innocent. The look of disappointment and betrayal that she wore etched now into my mind for all eternity. It was my vision that was coming true as they led her to the stake, burning her alive, just as I had foreseen. As hurt as she looked, my sister did not protest, she did not attempt to ensure that I suffered the same fate. As soon as the pyre was lit, I knew though, I finally understood that if one of us were good and one evil, it was not her that should be on that stake.

Too ashamed to return to the farm, I fled across fields and valleys, making my way through the woodland until I came across a ramshackle home which had been deserted for many years. It is from this place that I am now destined to live out my existence alone. The visions still come, more frequently than I would like, but I have no inclination to share them with the world for fear of meeting the same end as my sister did all those years ago. It is a curse that I will have to endure throughout all time, along with the unbearable guilt, taking it to my grave.

DREAM CATCHER

It was brand new technology, an adaptation of those sports watches which monitor how well a person sleeps. It was so completely new, in fact, that they were still in the trial phase. Being keen on both fitness and gadgets, it was only to be expected that Paul had purchased each latest model of watch as they were released. At the bottom of one email from his favourite brand, there was an invitation to take part in the beta-testing phase of the newest design. Paul had signed up to apply without a second thought, after all he was the ideal customer to test such a thing.

The new model was being temporarily referred to as D2V by the manufacturers - Dreams to Visual. From a fitness point of view, it had the same functions that his other watches had had; heart rate, step counter, sleep duration and, of course, time and date. These could all be viewed on the watch's screen and via an app on Paul's smart phone. The key difference, and it was a big one, was the dream function. It was being marketed as being able to record your dreams, with the goal being to establish the possible causes of them. However, the real deal-breaker was the playback function. Recording the pattern of brain activity whilst a person slept, the software could formulate the dream into a visual piece. Essentially, you could watch your dreams when you were awake, like a film.

It was unclear whether or not testers for these samples were chosen at random, or whether Paul's spiel about how he was the perfect candidate had held any sway, but he was chosen as one of five people to take part in the testing phase. The watch was to be dispatched to arrive the following day, and the confirmation email contained a link to the app, from which he could install it on his phone, as the app was not yet publicly available. Paul immediately installed the application, and it was clear that there was still some work to do on its presentation. There was a dashboard, as with the other fitness apps he had used, but currently this only featured the sleep and dream information. As this was the newest technology, it made sense that this should be found to be working as intended before adding the other, simpler, features. From what Paul could tell, the app would record how long he had slept for and any time spent awake or restless, as well as any dream itself. There was a video camera icon on the screen to push when he wished to view his dream from the previous night. Paul found it all hugely intriguing and eagerly awaited delivery.

The next day the watch arrived, looking much the same as any other. It bore the time and date on the rather large face, but all features were disabled bar the dream recording. Alison, Paul's wife tried to show an interest, relieved that he had not spent more money on a device that he did not really need, but she was becoming bored with hearing about how many steps he had taken each day. The dream recording sounded far-fetched to Alison and, despite doubting that it would actually work, she teased him about how she would now know if he had been dreaming about other women. This got Paul's back up, having not found the joke amusing, and he pointed out that he did not remember the last time he had a dream about anything. *What are you testing it for then?* Alison asked him, innocently enough. Paul did not answer, however, deciding to read through the chart that he had been sent with the watch to complete.

It looked fairly straightforward, with boxes to fill in with the date, length of sleeping and basic information that the manufacturers would be able to take from the app anyway. The one box that was extra to the logged information was named 'side effects'. Paul was to write in there if he felt different in any way, whether this was sickness, headaches and so on. *Guess they're just covering themselves,* he thought. The day dragged on and, with the help from a bottle of red wine, Paul finally felt ready to get to sleep. *Let's see what this thing does then.*

The morning arrived with the shriek of his alarm, and Paul sleepily reached across to silence it. He always set his for around an hour before Alison awoke, his intention being to go on a run before she was up. This happened on approximately half of the mornings, which he saw as still quite an achievement. As much as the wine had helped him to sleep, his head ached a little and the thought of leaving the bed was too much at that moment. Glancing at the watch around his wrist, he quickly remembered the dream recorder and decided to test it out before his wife was there looking over his shoulder. *I don't remember dreaming anything,* he thought glumly, expecting there to be nothing to view.

The dashboard on the app showed a video, only three minutes in length. *Well, I suppose it wouldn't run for the same length of time that I was sleeping,* he thought, contemplating how time appears to distort in one's dreams. Taking his earphones from the side of the bed, Paul inserted them into the socket and hit play. The video was jumpy, like a badly edited film. The whole thing appeared to be from his point of view, or at least, someone whom he assumed was himself. He watched as he got into a black car, a large one that he did not recognize. The scene jumped to him walking through an empty city at night, then through a green door at the side of an unmarked building. Suddenly, Paul found himself in some sort of underground nightclub, possibly the interior of the building he had just entered, perhaps somewhere else entirely. It looked similar to something he had seen in a film recently and assumed that this was where the thought had originated.

As the video continued, Paul saw himself approach the bar and the scenes merged into one blurry tale. He was downing shots of an amber liquid, flashing lights cutting through the darkness inside the room to illuminate the crowd. Suddenly, two women appeared beside him, looking as though they were talking to him, but he could not hear them over the music. Dressed in tight leather and with multiple piercings, they began kissing each other as Paul stared on and then, for an unknown reason, they wrote a telephone number on a book of matches bearing the club's logo of an upside-down cross with an eye above it. It was as one of the women, the one with the large spider tattoo on her neck, handed him the number, the video ended. *Bloody alarm clock!* Paul thought.

He struggled to understand the video and, apart from being glad that Alison had not watched it, he did not know what to think. He certainly did not remember having that dream, but he had read somewhere that we dream every night, usually completely forgetting it, by the time we awaken. While the dream was fresh on his mind, Paul decided to fill out the feedback sheet with the data and get himself ready for the day, having enjoyed the video and becoming more intrigued to see what tomorrow's would look like.

Alison was not working that day and had

barely risen when Paul was ready to leave for work. He bid her good-bye before she had chance to ask about any dreams and made his way out to his car only to find himself blocked in. The car was parked outside their house, as usual, but he had left it with the rear bumper close to the front of the one behind. Some inconsiderate sod had parked in front of his, in the identical fashion that he had. Most of the cars on their street were the same ones each day, and he had a good idea of who owned which. This one was different though; it looked out of place but strangely familiar. *Maybe someone bought a new car?* he wondered, seeing that he would not get out of the space with the big, black 4x4 in the way. The car behind belonged to the lady who lived next door, so he knocked for her, hoping that she would be able to move it for him. After a few attempts, there still came no answer, and he unhappily wandered along to the nearest bus stop, calling his workplace to forewarn them of his inevitable lateness.

The bus journey felt as though it was taking much longer than usual, something that often happens when one is in a hurry. It was the same route as he had taken many times before, in the days prior to owning the car, but there were parts that looked different somehow. *I haven't taken a bus for a while,* he thought. *I'm sure it's nothing.* It was only when he stood up to get off of the bus that he felt a hand grab his arm. Turning suddenly, he saw an elderly man holding on to him.

"You dropped this," he told Paul, opening his hand slowly. Paul's eyes widened as he looked at the black match book, cross and eye logo featured on the front of it. Quickly, Paul snatched it from the man and stuffed it into his pocket without so much as a thank you. It was too much to process, making no sense at all. Had he actually dropped it? If so, how did he come to even have it? Heading down a narrow walkway as a short cut to the office, he paused to open the matches. Inside was a telephone number, just as he had seen in the video. He decided, as he was already late for work, to replay the footage and try to make sense of it. *The car!* Paul saw that the car from his dream looked almost identical to the one outside his house. The matches were also the same. *But where was this club? And those women?!*

Trying not to panic, Paul asked around about nightclubs, as casually as he could manage. It didn't come naturally for him, his years of clubbing having long since passed and the gothic, metal scene was not one with which his co-workers would associate him with. No-one seemed to know of the place he was describing, having told them that it was somewhere Alison had suggested that they go one evening. The day moved slowly, even after being an hour late to work. The only contact he had had from Alison was a text asking him why he had not taken the car. Paul told her that it had been blocked in by 'some idiot with a 4x4' and that next door were not home. Apparently, the car was gone by the time Alison had looked outside.

Paul chose not to mention the dream video or the matches as he was unable to explain of it. There was a strong temptation to call the number on the matches but, as foolish at it sounded, he was scared to. He did, however, decide to write on the feedback form about these strange occurrences in the 'side effects' column. As impossible as they seemed, there had to be some kind of connection. Before bed on that second night, Paul decided to watch the video one more time in the hope that his dream would continue from where it had left off. *Perhaps something about the club's location will be revealed? Maybe something to identify the women?*

When morning came, once again his sleep interrupted by his alarm, there was another video. This was a longer one, nearer to five minutes. Whether or not it continued on from the previous footage was impossible to say, the time line in dreams not being as linear as in real life. There were similarities between the two clips, however, especially the 'feel' of them. If they had been movies, they would have looked as though they had had the same director. The second dream was more surreal than the first and featured Paul apparently stumbling across some kind of secret society preparing for a ritual of sorts. It was, again, very jumpy and Paul saw winding tunnels, torches of fire adorning the walls. There was a line of people passing him as he wandered along them, all in red gowns with their hoods up. No one was speaking. As soon as the last person passed him Paul turned to join the end of the procession, looking down to see that he too was wearing a red gown. He followed them through to a large chamber, hundreds of candles illuminating it. A huge stone pentacle was embedded into the rock beneath his feet as he gazed upon a marble table that was by now encircled by the other people. On the table was a woman, fully nude, face down. Her ankles and wrists were tied to poles, spreading them as far as she could manage. From where Paul stood, her head was farthest from him, affording him a rather explicit view.

Terrified at what appeared to be about to happen, Paul turned to try and leave. His path was blocked, however, by a female figure. The red hood masked most of the features on her face, only a large tattoo of a spider being visible on her neck. It was at this moment of finding some familiarity that his alarm clock must dragged him back to reality, and the video ended suddenly. *This is fucking weird,* he thought, not having the slightest memory of any dream, especially ones like these. Today Paul did feel sick, which he put down to the general state of confusion that he was in. Nevertheless, once he had had the idea that he should call work and take a day off; it was decided. Alison would be leaving within an hour or so and then he could try to get to the bottom of what was happening. Once the bathroom was free, Paul opted to take an excessively long shower, hoping that his wife would not think of asking if the watch had captured any dreams yet. He told her that he was feeling a bit funny and not going to work. She looked at him suspiciously, knowing full well that he was fine and wondering what he was up to. Alison chose to say nothing and, after giving him a peck on the forehead, left the house to go to work.

Time to man up, Paul thought as he began to dial the number from the book of matches. There was no answer but it went to an answering service, a woman's voice telling him to leave a message, and she *might* get back to him. He chose not to, unable to think of anything to say. He certainly couldn't think of anything believable anyway. Wandering around the house in just his towel, Paul tried to decide what he should do. He thought about calling the people who had sent him the watch but doubted they would have anything useful to say; they'd probably think he was insane if anything. He regretted not taking the number plate of the 4x4 and now had no way to try to follow up on that potential clue. Turning to the Internet for help, Paul began searching for clubs that sounded similar to the one he had seen. There were none anywhere near to wear he lived, the nearest rock and metal clubs being more than an hour away. He had no luck finding the logo either and started to read up on sacrificial rituals, desperate to find a solid link. *Of course, it could just be constructed from my mind, dreaming something doesn't make it real,* he told himself, trying to ignore the fact that the matches on his kitchen table were indeed very much existent.

The information that he found online was tedious and very general, mostly referring to suspected rituals carried out by various groups, but with nothing confirmed as being accurate. There were no known groups which wore red gowns and sacrificed women, assuming that was their intention, above the symbol of the pentacle. After two mugs of coffee and no real progress, Paul made his way back upstairs to get dressed. Opening his wardrobe, he almost missed it at first, pulling a T-shirt off of a hanger. Changing his mind on the choice of clothing, he went to hang it back up when he saw it. It would be more accurate to say he felt it before actually laying eyes on it, the softness standing out as unfamiliar. Hands beginning to tremble, Paul slowly removed the red, hooded gown from his wardrobe, the sickness that he had felt earlier becoming a full-on wave of nausea.

Paul threw the gown on to his bed, along with the matches, and stared at them. To begin with he felt confused, muddled. Now he felt terrified, more so than he had ever been before. *It has to be a prank,* he told himself, hopefully. *But it's not fucking funny if someone is coming in my house!* Angrily, Paul redialed the number from the matches and this time, left a message. *I don't know what's going on, but it needs to stop now. You've had your fun.* Having been unable to shout at an actual person, Paul still felt on edge and chose to call the manufacturers of the watch. The customer service adviser did not sound remotely concerned or surprised by what Paul told her. She explained patiently that the software had created a visual record of his dreams, and it was perfectly normal to see things from these dreams when awake, but that these were coincidences. After all, she had said, there are probably thousands of black 4x4s. Paul tried to explain, as calmly as he could, that the gown which had appeared in his wardrobe was not there before. He only saw it in the dream. *Perhaps it's your wife's and you didn't know she had it,* was all he was told. Accepting that he was getting nowhere he finished the call without saying good-bye.

Soon realizing that Paul would know nothing further until the watch had recorded some more footage, he became desperate for the night to come. It was barely lunchtime and he felt helpless as he waited, frightened of what was to come next. There were still at least six or seven hours until Alison would be home, and then it came to him, an idea that was definitely worth a try. A few months ago, after a bout of quite severe depression, Alison had been prescribed temazepam. Paul recalled how they would render Alison asleep within half an hour, sending her off for a good four to five hours if she only took one. He reasoned that, as he was supposed to be ill anyway, it wouldn't seem too strange should he be in bed when she returns and grabbing a bottle of water from the fridge, he decided to take two of the pills and get into bed.

Taking one pill would have been more sensible it seemed, nine hours having passed whilst Paul slept. He awoke groggy, a little confused from sleeping during the daytime. Once he saw how long he had been out for he made his way downstairs to find his wife but she was not there. Glancing out of the living room window, he could not see her car parked anywhere nearby either. *Strange,* he thought and went back upstairs to get his phone. Seeing no messages from his wife to explain her absence, he prepared himself to view the latest dream footage, scared of what he would see.

The dream had continued, exactly from the point at which the last had ended. Paul stood in the red robe, gazing at the face of the woman he had met in the bar. No one spoke; the only sound within the room was the stifled murmurs of the woman tied to the table. Paul turned back to look at the naked victim, watching her writhe about in an attempt to get free. Her head was covered by a mask of some sort, similar to the kind worn at nineteenth-century dances. He watched as someone broke from the circle and approached the victim, something glowing in their hand. It was only as they rose it into the air that Paul saw that it was a branding iron. Helplessly he looked on as the upturned cross and the all-seeing eye were burnt into the woman's back. Paul quickly turned to leave, attempting to overpower the tattooed woman, but to no avail.

Despite there being no conversation, something propelled him to act. It was a form of acceptance, as though he knew what was expected of him, and he felt that the consequence for refusing far outweighed the terrible act that he was to perform. Sitting on his bed, Paul watched as he moved forward in the video, standing directly behind the bound woman. The film was jumpy again so it was unclear as to where the knife had come from, but it was now in his hand, and he had to do as requested. Raising the blade into the air with both hands around the handle, he plunged it into the woman's back repeatedly. He heard a cracking sound as it hit bone, sticky scarlet spurts emanating from the gashes he was leaving on her. Viciously, infinitely more so than he could imagine himself being capable of, he kept stabbing, repeatedly, until all he could see was red. As he looked around at the others who had watched him, they began to clap. The applause grew and grew, echoing from the cavern walls. Then it ended, just like that.

After finding the matches and now the gown, it should not have been too surprising when he found something else, which did not belong. Only this time, it sort of did. The knife was his, from the block in the kitchen. The blood, however, could have been anyone's. Fear set in once again, dreading what had happened, terrified of what would be coming next. *Would this all stop if I just take the watch off?,* he wondered. Unable to think of anything else to try, he removed the watch and attempted to call his wife. The call went straight to voice mail. It was too late to call her workplace, so he would have to wait. Being alone and frightened was not good, and he hoped that Alison would be back soon so that he could tell her what was going on, perhaps she could help somehow.

The sound of the doorbell interrupted his train of thought and, without considering why Alison would not have just let herself in, he headed to answer, relieved to have her home. The four police officers at his door came as a shock, fearing that something had happened to his wife. With little explanation, Paul was cuffed and led to a waiting police car while the other officers made their way into his home. The conviction was solid; the police having found the knife covered in Alison's blood as well as video footage of the ceremony itself. She was found down an alleyway, outside a green door. Apart from a mask, she was fully nude and, among the seventy-four stab wounds to her back, there were the remnants of some satanic symbol burnt into her skin. There were traces of hair and fibres from both himself, and Alison discovered in the back of a black 4x4 hire car, registered under his name. His version of what had happened was laughed away, no one believing in a dream catching watch or any of the other oddness surrounding the case. The more he protested his innocence, the less anything made sense and Paul was deemed to be delusional, not to mention extremely dangerous. He was never to be released from the psychiatric facility and would spend the rest of his days in his own room, the only human interaction coming when his meals were delivered by the pretty girl with the spider tattoo on her neck.

EMBRACE THE DARKNESS

I was around seven or eight when I first had a nightmare. At least, that was the initial one which was vivid enough that I can still recall it. It was short, not a lot of detail being provided in my mind. I saw myself lying upon the bed in my small room and there, in the farthest corner, between the top of the wall and the ceiling, was the creature. It had formed a kind of nest, strings of white hanging from the ceiling as it nestled there, web-like entrails surrounding its dark form. In my dream, I could not see it properly. It appeared just as a shape, but the terror which I felt that night is something that I remember well. I did not sleep in my own bedroom for a number of weeks after that night.

When I was fourteen, I awoke in the early hours of the morning, screaming. My sleep had been interrupted by another nightmare, a continuation from the one I had had all those years previously. I was still sleeping in the same bedroom. We had resided at the house all of my life, only my bed was on the opposite side of the room at this point. The monster, however, was back in its original spot, now appearing directly above me and this time it had begun to move. I recall the dream as clearly as I do the previous one. I remember, in my dream state, gazing up at the creature and thinking, *'That's the same monster from my dream before!'* It was a feeling of wonderment, rather than fear, to begin with. That was until it started to shift, an almost human-like face unfurling, jet black in its entirety except for two pupil-less, perfectly round, white eyes. As the terrifying face began to push against the web which it had created for itself, I screamed, waking from the nightmare as I sat upright in bed.

My fourteen-year-old-self was more able to accept that it had only been a nightmare, but I still felt uneasy each night, desperately trying to think about other things before sleep took me. No sooner had I managed to banish the dream from my mind, then I had another one, yet again the same. It was only the briefest moment, that awful face continuing to press against the web as if it were trying to come closer to me, but the level of terror that I felt was enough to begin affecting me during my waking hours. I would see the creature in a whole host of places, more and more often as the weeks went by. My family thought that I was suffering from arachnophobia at one point due to the way that I would recoil from the sight of a spider on its web. Shadows in the corners of rooms would take the form of that face, nowhere felt safe.

Between the ages of fifteen and twenty, it haunted me. I saw it almost daily, regardless of where I was it would find a way to reveal its face. The constant torment had serious repercussions for my mental well being, resulting in a dependency on anti-anxiety medication as well as, on the insistence of my doctor, some experimentation with anti-psychotics. I blamed my childhood bedroom. I longed to sleep anywhere but there and so, at the age of sixteen, I left. My family understood, to a point, my reasoning, but they were frightened for me. It was not as though they believed that there was anything dangerous about the dream itself, of course, but they could see how my mental health was deteriorating so rapidly.

I found a small room not far from home, renting from a man who was mostly away on business, thus leaving the whole house to me. I thought it would be perfect; I thought I would be safe there. Nevertheless, the dreams became more regular still, each visualization bringing the creatures cracked, blackened face closer to mine. I became dangerously close to the edge of existence, feeling the immense pull of both anxiety and depression. My mind was a constant battle between being too frightened to leave the house and too afraid to stay in it. I never knew if I wanted to be alone, or if I needed company, I found it difficult to distinguish between what was real and what was not.

As much as I struggled, I managed to hold down a job, and I managed to control, what the doctor had called, my symptoms. There were specific places which I had to avoid, such as dark alleyways and suspicious-looking marks along the sides of buildings, and this caused me to take the long way to and from work each day. I did not dare to tell my colleagues, most of whom I would drink with after work, for fear that they would ridicule me, and so I suffered my burden for months on end, positive that one night the creature would finally reach me.

In my dreams, I was always back in the bedroom at my family home, the dream being virtually identical each horrific time that it came to me. It had been devastating that my plan to live elsewhere had not helped and now, regardless of anything, that thing was etched so deeply into my mind that it had become a part of me. I wanted it to go, to leave me in peace, but it would not. I searched for help, sure that there must be a way of erasing the memory, but there was nothing. All I could do was embrace it, fight the feeling of gut-wrenching dread and not pay it any attention. This was what I had decided and, as hard as it was, I began to face my fear. I started to take the more direct route to work, music blasting in my ears, eyes darting anywhere except where the shadows would lie. I'd stay awake for much longer than was healthy, pushing myself to the extreme until even the mix of caffeine and recreational drugs could not keep sleep at bay.

The dreams slowly started to subside, sleep having been replaced with a deeper level of unconsciousness, and I felt as though I was finally winning. That was how it had seemed to me, anyway. From the outside, I was a mess, sleeping only two or three hours each night, dependent on amphetamines, rarely eating. My parents were worried, making their disapproval of me ever so clear, and I reacted in the easiest way that I could; I stopped seeing them. I chose to do that rather than risk the nightmares returning. My friends and colleagues did not seem to see me as the disaster that my parents described me as, possibly because they were all a mess in their own ways. We were all young, we all wanted to the same kind of excitement and we all felt a need for escape.

On the approach to my twenty-first birthday, someone suggested we went camping, a group of us, to some woodland not far from home. It was always deserted, I was told. It could be fun, they all said. My anxiety kicked in at the thought of being in the woods, surrounded by that pitch black, enveloping darkness. I told them that I would think about it, tried to brush it off as 'camping not really being my thing'. However, they had made the decision, and they insisted that it would be great. There would be drinks, there would be drugs, so potentially I could stay awake all night. I'd have plenty of company; I would be safe. Peer pressure, being the thing that it is, gave me little choice when the day came around and so, with just a bag of essentials and a large torch, I made my way out with five others.

I was very self-aware; I had learned what triggered the fears, and I knew how to manage them to the best of my ability. I was also very keen on drugs but, for the sake of trying to cling to my last strands of sanity, I had avoided any hallucinogens. It sounded like an insane idea for me to try anything like that, I was seeing things far too often without the help of drugs. This is the reason I refused the mushrooms that night. Even so, I did not explain why. And this is the reason my friends gave me them anyway, without my knowledge. From what I had been told previously, hallucinations are all well and good provided you know that you've taken something. If you have no way of knowing that it is the drugs, rather than reality, things become much more sinister. Especially if your mind is already packed full of terrifying images.

We made a fire, sitting around it passing a couple of bottles of cheap scotch back and forth. I drank it, preferring that to the bloating, sleep-inducing effects of beer. I let the cannabis pass me, knowing from previous experiences that it would knock me out and, with a couple of pills inside me, avoiding looking into the darkness, I began to relax. One of the girls announced that she was going to get some snacks and wandered off to the pile of bags and coats that we had slung at the foot of a huge tree. The drugs had completely destroyed my appetite, and I could not face food, but as I tried to decline, she smiled so sweetly at me. Foolishly, I thought she was interested in me, coming back to the group with only a handful of pastry bites. She popped one in her mouth and held one up for me, her fingers running across my lips, my mouth opening. Two were all that I could manage and no sooner had I swallowed them then the girl began laughing. She made no explanation as to what had amused her so much and I, mistakenly, put it down to her drunkenness.

I was unaware of the hour, but it was late enough to be dark during the summer time, certainly approaching midnight at least. The cover of the trees and the remote location had created an eerie shadiness as night enveloped our merry group. I had lost track of the conversation, it having been centred around some band I had not heard of, and my eyes had begun to wander towards the trees. The clearing in which we were sat was small, aside from a little trail along which we had wandered, we were now completely surrounded by woodland, and I was starting to feel anxious.

The nearest trunks were only a few metres away from me, and I could detect their form as they stood, towering above us menacingly. Beyond the trunks was an inky blackness, nothing else being visible. Almost nothing. As I looked over the shoulder of the person sat opposite me, I noticed two white circles, a few feet from the ground, perfectly spherical and close enough to one another to be eyes. Pupilless eyes. I took a double take, trying to convince myself that it was just my mind playing tricks on me, that I was safe despite the threatening feel of my surroundings. On the second look, I could not see them, but then they were back, this time a few feet to the left of where they had been previously.

A look of fear must have been noticeable as my friends started to ask if I was alright, through little giggles and knowing smiles. I told them what I'd seen and, as amusing as they were finding my sense of dread, one of them confessed to the mushrooms. I was angry but tried to conceal it, terrified of embarrassing myself but equally convinced that what I had seen was real. If I was to be afraid, then so should they, as reprisal for their cruel prank. I began to talk about my dreams, the things that I had seen, theatrically telling the scary story around the campfire. I described the blackened face of my visitor, the bizarre form that it seemed to take, the sticky, imprisoning web that it formed.

Everyone listened intently, enjoying the tale. The guys laughed it off but the girls, more easily frightened, began scouring the tree line for anything out of place. In order to prove his bravery, or to reassure the girls, and myself that there was nothing to fear, the young man opposite me stood up and announced that he needed to take a piss and would be back soon. Unless the white-eyed monster gets me, he told us with a chuckle. We heard the crack of brittle twigs as he made his way into the darkness, the rest of us waiting in total silence for the sound of his return. He had not ventured far, and we could hear the splash of urine as it sprayed against a tree. Then we heard nothing. No more rustling leaves, no more crunching footsteps. Only silence.

Convinced that he was playing a prank on us, we began a new conversation, certain that he would get bored and reappear shortly. After a good ten minutes or so there was still no sign, and it became clear that we would need to investigate, something that not one of us was willing to do alone. My heart was racing, the terror, combined with the drugs, now pushing it to its limit. The girls began to call out for our missing friend, becoming angry that it could be a joke. It only took a few steps into the woodland before someone screamed. The rest of us, unable to see the gruesome spectacle, raced to get back to the clearing.

I had been at the back of our group and so was the first one to reach the fire. I turned around to see that we were now half the number we had been when we had arrived, just myself and two girls stood in shock. We called to the others to no avail but did not have the courage needed to return to the darkness to look for them. All we could hope to do was to grab our belongings and run, to try to find help. No sooner had they bent down to pick up our bags, then I saw it again, the eyes staring from the darkness. It all happened so quickly, the speed at which it claimed its prize was unexpected. In a matter of seconds, the creature had appeared, long, thin legs propelling it rapidly in circles around the tree that our bags were strewn beside. The white, tangled, sticky web sprayed from the end of its short, almost birdlike arms and after the shortest moment, it had bolted back into the night.

Silence fell once more, the girls now secured against the trunk of the tree by the creature's web. It had engulfed them with such force that they had been bent and twisted, limbs contorted at angles which were not usually possible, one of their heads suddenly facing the wrong way. If they had survived the envelopment, then suffocation would have surely taken them, but I had no doubt that they had met a quick, albeit horrific, demise.

I could not run, fear having fixed me to the spot, and I now knew that this is what had been waiting for me, it had been on its way since that first dream as a child. I stood beside the fire with my eyes closed and took a large gulp from the whiskey bottle. Embrace the darkness, I told myself. It seemed inevitable. I waited but there was nothing. I knew that the horrors which I had just seen would drive me over the edge, and I saw no way to go on living after this. I did not want to be the sole survivor, to have to face my fears day in and day out once again. Eventually, I opened my eyes, wondering why the beast had left me standing, only to meet the gaze of two white circles. The black, cracked face was inches from mine, a crooked smile having appeared revealing equally sooty teeth.

Simultaneously, the creature and I raised our arms and as the web began to fly from it, I held the rough, jet black skin in an embrace. I held it in my arms, feeling the tightening of the restraints as they bound us together, my lungs beginning to struggle for air. The monster and I became as one, cocooned with each other in inescapable bondage. I felt myself slip from consciousness, the only sound being the crack of my bones as I was crushed against the blackness of my nightmare. After years of torment, terror in every waking and sleeping moment, the creature had finally taken me. Even so, I had also taken it, and now we were both complete.

OPENED UP

The doctor had seemed more concerned about the lump than I had, having just shown it to her on the off-chance that it warranted taking action. A year, I told her. That was how long it had been noticeable, protruding from the top of my foot as though a golf ball had been stitched beneath the skin. It did not hurt, I explained, which is why I virtually ignored it all of this time. Recently, however, there had been a little discomfort when wearing shoes, as if the increased mass of my foot was now too much to fit inside my favourite brogues.

"We will need to do some tests," she told me, her eyes meeting mine as she tried to portray the seriousness of the situation.

"OK," I told her. "So what is it?"

"The chances are that it is harmless, most likely a ganglion cyst, and will have to be removed. Nevertheless, we need to arrange an ultrasound scan, to rule out anything more serious." *Cancer,* I realized, the thought having not entered my head thus far. I did my best over the next few days to keep any panic from my mind, having read online that the chances of it being a cancerous growth were less than two in one hundred. Even so, the doctors were incredibly efficient, and I received an appointment for the ultrasound within a week.

"Looks like a cyst," I was told as an implement was run across my bare foot, squelching through the cold jelly.

"It looks like a cyst, or it is one? Like, for definite," I asked, needing some clarification.

"It looks like a cyst," the ultrasound nurse repeated, this time taking his eyes from the monitor to look at me. "I would bet that it is a cyst. That said, there have been times that we've been wrong and not known until the surgeon starts taking it off. Either way, its got to go." I was told to expect an appointment for surgery very soon, most likely at a private facility due to the longer waiting lists at public hospitals.

Ten days later, I found myself sat in the waiting area of a small private hospital, on the surgery list of a Mr. Yambus. The morning, they told me. That was as specific as they could be, but I would be one golf ball sized lump lighter by midday. Due to the anesthetic, I was not to eat that day, and as I sat as patiently as I could, my stomach began to rumble. After almost four hours of pacing the waiting room and watching all the other patients disappear to theatre, I went to enquire about the holdup.

"Mr. Yambus is on his lunch break now; I'm afraid," the crow-faced receptionist told me.

"I'm supposed to be having an operation this morning. What time will it be then?"

"Take a seat, I'll find out." With that, the receptionist left her station and scurried away down the corridor. This is the point at which I should have felt that something was amiss, her absence for the next forty-five minutes being a good indicator. Three-quarters of an hour I spent sat in that room alone, no other patients, no visitors and, now, not even the receptionist. The only time I stood from my chair was to visit the toilet which was at one end of the room. If I had needed to venture further maybe I would have seen that all was not as it should have been. If I had attempted to go back out to the street, then I may well have panicked upon finding the large glass doors of the main entrance now locked. I remained blissfully unaware, only mildly irritated by the delay, more distraught by the lack of food.

Despite the strangeness of the situation, I played the part of the model patient, waiting as instructed. Finally, the receptionist returned. Physically, she appeared the same but there was something unfamiliar about her. I could not put my finger on it, only a sense that she had returned and was now different. Her voice was slower than before, her eyes not quite looking at me as she spoke.

"Sorry for the delay," she mumbled; her gaze just passing over my left shoulder. "The doctor is ready for you now. Follow me." She led me along the corridor from which she had appeared, arriving at a staircase to my left. I glanced up the stairs ahead of me and saw that the next floor was in darkness. As we began to ascend the stairs, the light fading, I had to ask the reason.

"Is there something wrong with the lights up here?"

"Not that I am aware of," she replied. "But it's an old building. It seems a little dim upstairs, I'm afraid." *A little dim!* I thought. *It's almost completely black!* At the top of the stairs, we passed through a doorway into a narrow corridor with drab, red carpets. The walls were painted in the repossessed house colour of magnolia with a hideous burgundy, floral border wallpapered along them. Damp patches appeared above the skirting boards, and all was eerily silent.

"This is your room," I was told, the words sounding almost robotic as they slowly struck my ears. "Get into the gown and I will be back soon."

I pushed to open the door to the private room, expecting the same level of darkness but my eyes were in for a shock. There was no issue with the lighting inside, the brilliance of it causing my pupils to retract suddenly. Once inside, I closed the door and looked around. It was spotlessly clean, as a hospital room should be, but in stark contrast to the corridor outside. There was a private bathroom and a hospital bed, a machine for taking observations, even a television fixed against the wall. The uneasy experience outside soon dissipated once inside, and I stripped out of my clothes, unsure whether or not to leave my underwear on beneath the gown that had been provided. I decided that, as the surgery was to be on my foot, there was no need for me to expose everything to the medical staff.

A few minutes later, as I struggled to drag the surgical stocking across my good foot, the receptionist returned and invited me to follow her once again, into the darkness of the corridor. We walked slowly through the darkness, my eyes following the line of wallpaper on either side of me. It was unexpectedly long, the hallway, and it was only as I started to feel we had walked further than I had anticipated, that I began to notice there had been no breaks in the wallpaper. No breaks and, therefore, no other doors which could have led to other rooms. As I weighed up whether or not to enquire about this oddity, the receptionist stopped suddenly. Slowly, she raised an arm, pointing ahead into the blackness.

"Take the lift down to level B, someone will meet you there." I could see no lift, or anything else up ahead, but I made my way cautiously regardless. *B?* I muttered, to myself. *As in basement?* I came across the shiny surface of the lift door and was relieved to find the inside of it was as brightly lit as my room had been. There was a choice of three buttons to press, 1, G and B. It was obvious that I was currently on level one, the first floor and, as unsettling as it sounded, I had to accept that level B was indeed the basement. In the short moments that the lift was in motion, I feared that I might step out into some horrific scene, some insane surgeon strapping patients to a metal table in the middle of a poorly lit room. This was not, however, the case.

I was greeted by a young woman as the lift doors parted. She spoke in broken English as she explained that she was the anesthetist and led me to a small room next door to the lift shaft.

"Do you have allergies?" she asked, her accent sounding as though she may be Polish, or Russian, perhaps. I told her that I did not have allergies, and she indicated to the bed, which I climbed upon, doing my best to keep my underwear covered.

"You feel a little prick," she told me, holding a long, thin syringe in one hand. My immature streak showed itself for a second as I let a little smile pass my lips at the words 'little prick'. As it happened, it was a rather sizable prick as I felt the needle pierce a substantial vein on the top of my left hand.

"Count backwards from ten," she ordered, placing a mask across my nose and mouth. "Out loud."

"Ten, nine, eight, seven..." and then I must have been gone. I could not say how long I was out for, only that when I came around I was back in the room, my room, tucked into the bed. The television was on, showing some kind of talk show and, sat in the chair with his back to me, was a man. I tried to speak but could not make a sound come out. *It must be the anesthetics,* I thought. I tried to move my arms but had no luck with that, either. This was the first time that I had had surgery, during my adult life, at least. I was unsure of what was normal and what was not so I waited, certain that I would regain some sensation shortly. It felt like an age before the man turned towards me, and if I had been physically able to, I may well have recoiled from the sight of his face.

He instantly reminded me of a comic book villain, severe burns causing the left-hand side of his face and neck to appear discoloured and lumpy. His left eye was no longer present and, rather than opting to wear any form of eye-patch, his face featured a gaping black hole instead.

"How is the patient feeling?" he asked, in a voice much more well-spoken and confident than I had expected. I could not answer, my mouth barely moving. "Ah, yes. You won't be able to speak yet; I'm afraid. Can you blink?" I tried blinking and found this to be manageable. "One for yes, two for no. Are you feeling alright?" *Of course not! I can't move or talk!* I blinked twice. "I see," he said, seemingly unsurprised. "Well, I'm Doctor Yambus," he told me. "I performed your operation. That was quite a lump you had there! However, I'm afraid I have a bit of bad news." My eyes felt wide, worried about what was coming next. "It turned out that the lump, which we had hoped was simply a ganglion cyst, was actually an egg. Rather unusual, I would say. Nevertheless, don't worry, we dealt with it, and all those little buggers which came spewing out as soon as the scalpel hit it!" The doctor said this with a chuckle, as if what he was telling me was an amusing anecdote that he was sharing at a cocktail party. My mind raced, wanting to know more about what had happened yet unable to speak. I attempted to concentrate my mind onto the foot, to try to detect anything out of the ordinary but there was nothing. Terror began to creep in as I realized that I could not feel any parts of my body.

"I bet you'd like to start feeling again," the doctor declared, as if he had read my mind. "Even so, trust me, you won't want to just yet. Would you like to watch the surgery? We record all of our procedures for the medical students; I can put it on for you if you'd like?" I paused, unsure if I really wanted to see my foot being cut open. *If I have no way of looking at my actual foot, then I suppose it's my only choice,* I thought. I blinked once.

"Jolly good," the doctor said, a sly look appearing across his face. "I have some things to attend to so I'll leave you to it." Once he had pressed some buttons on the televisions remote, the doctor left the room, leaving me to view the gruesome reality of what I had been through. The video began with my unconscious body being wheeled into an operating theatre by the young anesthetist. I appeared as I expected to look, the mask still attached to my face, the hospital gown covering my body, one surgical stocking in place. The first few minutes showed the doctor making preparations as he painted my foot with an orange liquid, drawing a line across the lump with black marker pen which I presumed to indicate the planned incision line. I was surprised that there were no other medical staff present, and as I pondered this, I watched the doctor move towards my foot with the scalpel. *An egg?!* I wondered, trying to convince myself that I had misheard him. However, I had not. I watched with widening eyes as the blade opened up the top of my foot, a jet of thick black liquid squirting from the newly formed entrance. If I had been able to gasp, that would have been the time to do it.

There was no sound on the video, so I could not tell if the doctor had anything to say, but he did keep looking toward the camera. With a length of dressing, he cleaned away the black mess until the opening was more visible, before beginning to scrape out the contents of the growth. It was next that I saw what he meant, the little buggers. One, then another, then a handful more. Small, black bugs of some description came jumping out of the wound, I would guess that they were the size of little flies. No sooner had they landed on the surrounding skin than they seemed to disappear again. It took me a moment to realize that they had not disappeared at all, instead they had immediately burrowed their way back inside me. More and more emerged from the opening, reaching further up my leg before disappearing from sight.

The doctor turned toward the camera once again, but I could not hear what was being said. As he turned back to his patient, a frenzy appeared to take over him as he tried to rid me of the infestation. Scalpel in hand, he stabbed at my legs, digging holes as he tried to coax the creatures out of my body. I watched in horror as he inflicted the wounds, my gown beginning to turn a terrifying shade of red. I lost count of the times that my skin had been pierced. The doctor turned toward the stainless steel table beside him and picked up a pair of scissors, proceeding to cut my gown down the middle. He pulled both sides away so that they hung from each side of my bed as he eyed my bare chest. It looked as though he was checking for any signs that I had been bored into by whatever had made a home inside my foot and, just when I thought that it was all clear, he launched another ferocious attack, dotting my whole body with shallow wounds.

Finally, as I lie there soaked in blood, a gaping black hole in my foot, the doctor appeared to be satisfied. He took one last look at the camera before choosing the hacksaw from the table. If it was not for my paralysis, I imagine that I would have vomited as I watched him remove my foot, placing it into a clear plastic bag. He disappeared off camera for a moment, carrying my foot with him, and returned with the anesthetist. They spoke to one another briefly, as he pointed out the wounds that he had inflicted on me. I watched her nodding in agreement to whatever she was being told, before walking away. Then the video ended and I lay there, in shock.

I could not move my body. I could not feel anything and worse than this, I could not even see the damage that had been done as I was unable to remove the duvet. The video had only been ended for a minute or two before the doctor returned to the room.

"Are you OK?" he asked, somewhat stupidly. I blinked twice. "I know it's a lot to take in. There's no hurry. Let me explain what has happened." The doctor continued to stand above me, his deformed face staring into my paralyzed one. "As you saw, you had an infestation. It's rare, but it does happen. We've taken a sample from you, as you could see." *That was my foot, not a bloody sample!* I thought, unable to say it aloud. "Unfortunately, these little critters are rather hardy, not all that easy to kill; you see. Which is why we've had to take some precautions, to stop them spreading to the outside world." My mind struggled from this point on as the doctor explained that I had to be given a drug, one I had not heard of, which effectively prevented me from being able to move, or feel. He had to tell me three times before I understood that this was now permanent. "You are a host," he told me, seeming to relish the condition that I had somehow found myself suffering from. "Which is why we need to keep you here."

Briefly, Dr Yambus disappeared from sight, returning from the bathroom with a mirror that he had removed from the wall. He looked at my eyes with his one eye as he held the mirror above me. It was angled as such that I could see my chest.

"You see?" he asked. I looked at the reflection, taking in the numerous wounds, now coated in dried blood. However, this was not the worst of it for they would heal. Spread across my chest were four lumps, much smaller than the one that had been on my foot, but clearly there and undoubtedly growing. If one had been enough to amputate my foot, I knew then that I could not survive this.

"Get some rest," the doctor told me, grinning as though he took pleasure in my predicament. "We may need to operate shortly."

THE DEVIL'S POCKET WATCH

Tess had always kept it secure, ever since her grandmother had entrusted her with it. *It was a great responsibility,* she had been told. As with anything that seemed to be lacking in evidence, Tess had been doubtful about its power, but she would not need to wait long to get the proof that she needed. She had never known her grandmother to lie; not about anything. She had also always appeared right minded and rational, not being drawn into the religious observations that had control over the rest of their family. Tess's mother, on the other hand, was not sane. She was also, by the time that Tess had turned fourteen, not alive either. It was not as if Tess had suffered some horrific childhood, raised solely by a mother now rarely spoken of it had just been a very conservative upbringing. This boiled down to virtually any pleasurable activity being viewed as a sin and, therefore, strictly prohibited.

For the first fourteen years of Tess's life, her grandmother was there as a person of comfort to her. Their bond strengthened considerably as Tess entered her teenage years, the changes to her body and mind becoming difficult for her mother to cope with. *It's as if she was never a teenage girl,* Tess thought on many occasions. Having at no time been allowed to date, or to stay out as late as her limited number of friends were, or to utter the intermittent profanity if she was to stub a toe, Tess yearned for rebellion. She had vented to her friends at school almost every day, jealous of how much more reasonable their parents appeared to be. She was coming to an age where spending time with her peers was much more important to her than spending time with her mother; she was finding her place in the world.

Tess's mother was repetitive in her warnings, trying to assure her daughter that the rules were in place for a good reason; *safety*. This was always the reason that was given and, perhaps if this was the only reason, then Tess could have accepted things in a more understanding way. Safety was not the main reason for her mother's rules and whenever a disagreement ensued, it was made perfectly clear that if Tess did not follow her mother's directions, then her soul would be spending eternity in a fiery pit.

"I'd take that over living with you!" Tess retorted on one occasion, and only one. Convinced that the Devil himself was speaking through Tess, her mother dealt with the statement in, what she called, a controlled manner. Tess's knuckles had turned purple from the wooden spoon that her mother had taken to her on that day, and she learned not to talk back from that point on. She also learned that her mother was a hypocrite; spouting on about 'loving thy neighbour' yet willing to attack her own child.

Three months after the assault, (this is what Tess, dramatically, called the incident), her mother was dead. It was ruled a suicide, ingestion of some kind of toxin. Despite this conclusion being reached, there were no traces found on the toxicology report. Tess did not see the body; her grandmother would not allow it, and this was certainly for the best. Tess was aware that her mother had been found lying across the bed, as stiff as a board. Her throat had been swollen up, causing suffocation. Her neck was red and raw with bloody scratch marks, self-inflicted from her clawing at it. Her eyes were wide open when Tess's grandmother had discovered the body, bulging almost out of their sockets. The coroner had decided that the injuries were consistent with a neurotoxin which causes a reaction similar to anaphylactic shock. This suggestion, coupled with the revelation that her mother had been taking anti-psychotic medication for a number of years and no evidence of foul play, led to the ruling of suicide.

"I really don't understand it," Tess had told her grandmother on the day of the funeral. *"She thought that suicide was a mortal sin, unforgivable. I just don't see that she would do it. Even if she wanted to."* Her grandmother said nothing, and although she looked sad, she smiled at Tess and held her close. It was an upsetting day, of course, as most funerals inevitably are. Once it was over, however, things started to get

better for Tess and ignoring the crushing feelings of guilt, which crept up on her regularly, she knew that she was happier now that her mother had gone.

Being raised by her grandmother was far more pleasant and as she was essentially a well behaved child, the two of them got on well. They compromised when Tess wanted to make plans that weren't immediately agreed to. Her grandmother gave her just enough freedom to learn from her mistakes and could see that this approach worked wonders to quell the rebellious nature that had been brewing in her granddaughter. Tess found that she wanted to spend time with her new guardian; enjoying her company and even, sometimes, turning down invitations from friends to stay home and hear her stories.

On the day that Tess turned eighteen, her grandmother woke her with breakfast. On the tray, next to a plate of warm eggs, were two items; a small box and an envelope. Tess opened the envelope first, expecting it to be only a birthday card. Instead, Tess also found a cheque. A much larger cheque than expected one, at that.

"It's not to all go on drinks!" she had been told playfully. Tess moved on to the box and the item inside took her breath away. Among the tissue paper sat a pocket watch, more intricately designed than she could have imagined to be possible.

"It's beautiful!" Tess told her grandmother as she flipped open the cover to reveal the watch's face.

"It's special. I need to talk to you about it," her grandmother replied, her voice taking on a more serious tone. She looked a little frightened. *"The watch was given to me by my mother, and she was given it by her mother. It has been passed from mother to eldest daughter for centuries; I have no idea how many generations now."*

"Why did you not give it to my mother then?" Tess asked, a little confused that the tradition had been broken.

"It is no ordinary watch, and your mother would not have been a suitable guardian for it. It requires a, shall we say, sounder mind to ensure that it is kept safe."

"I'm sorry Grandma," Tess began, trying to phrase her question delicately. *"Are you saying it's magical in some way??"* Her grandmother just nodded slowly. *"And yet,"* Tess continued, *"You say my* mother *was not sane enough to look after it?"*

"I see your point, and magical is possibly not the best word for it. I have a duty to explain it all, and I am more than aware of how crazy it sounds at first. The story goes that the watch once belonged to your very distant relation, Polly Matthews. This is going back many hundreds of years, of course. Polly was burned at the stake, a

common practice at the time, for being a witch. Whether or not she was a witch is impossible to say, they would burn people for having an epileptic seizure in those days! The tale has been passed on for generations, that the watch once belonged to the Devil himself, and that it has the power to claim souls for hell."

"Right," Tess stated, sarcastically. *"Well it's a good yarn Grandma. And it really is a lovely watch.* Tess's grandmother just stared at her, silently. *"You don't actually believe that, do you?"* Tess asked, incredulously. *"I mean, you can't!"*

"I didn't at first, well I suppose I never really did for a long time. I mean, I used the watch each day and, as far as I can tell, it hasn't whisked my soul off to eternal damnation! Nevertheless, something happened; I suppose it pretty much confirmed the story for me. Paradoxically, now that I know what it can do I will never be able to look in its face again."

Tess stared blankly, wondering why her sane and rational grandmother was now talking about demonic watches.

"You're making no sense at all. And you're giving me the creeps a bit too so can I just eat my eggs please. Thank you for the money, what should I spend it on?" Tess asked, trying to change the subject.

"I don't want you to believe me, you shouldn't really. You just need to trust me enough to make

sure it's kept safe and that no-one other than you uses it. Promise me, please," her grandmother pleaded.

"So, let me try to get this straight," Tess said, a little impatiently. *"It's only unsafe if you believe it is, therefore, it's safe for me because I don't. However, despite not believing that it's dangerous, I'm to treat it as though it were? And if that's the case, what happened to make you think this thing has some kind of unexplainable power?"*

"I can't tell you. I'm sorry. If I did, and you accepted what I said as truth, then I would be putting you in danger. Can you just promise me that you'll keep it safe? It's a lovely watch, there is no reason for you not to look after it regardless of the reasons."

"Of course, I'll keep it safe, and obviously I'll pass it on to my daughter if I ever have one. However, I think you might be going a little senile in your old age," Tess teased. *"It really is harmless, see."* As she uttered these words, Tess flipped open the cover to reveal that clock face and pointed it directly at her grandmother. Before she had a chance to look away, the elderly lady began to gasp for breath, her weak, arthritic hands clawing at her throat as it swelled. There was almost no time to act and by the time Tess had thrown her tray of breakfast to one side and jumped out of bed her grandma had taken her last breath.

Tess now believed, for it was too great a coincidence to not be true. The part about the soul being dragged off to hell still seemed far-fetched but there was no doubting that something evil was lurking within the watch. Fearful of meeting the same fate, Tess guarded the watch at all times, too afraid to open it herself. The circumstances surrounding her mother's death weighed heavy upon her mind for many years to come, as Tess deliberated what had actually happened. She would never know for certain but this may have been for the best. After all, there had been enough trauma in Tess's young life already. Knowing that, propelled by an inclination to improve her grandchild's life, as well as a curiosity about the trinket she had guarded for almost fifty years, Tess's grandmother had deliberately cast her own daughter's soul into the pit and inadvertently sealed the same fate for herself, would have been an unbearable burden. Tess did, however, manage to live a long life with one drawback. She was barren, there was no way around it, and there was to be no-one to pass on the watch to.

It's a sign, she thought, distraught by the state of the world with its wars and destruction. As the end of her life approached, Tess took the watch to an antique's store and placed it among the other items without attracting anyone's attention. *The Devil can take as many souls as he wants now.*

Printed in Great Britain
by Amazon